I wish I were...

a princess

Ivan Bulloch & Diane James

In association with
FRANKLIN WATTS

Created by Two-Can Publishing Ltd
346 Old Street
London EC1V 9NQ

Art Director Ivan Bulloch
Editor Diane James
Design Assistant Lisa Nutt
Illustrator Dom Mansell
Photographer Daniel Pangbourne
Models Courtney, Natalia, Shelby, Jonathan,
Grant, Kaz, Abigail, Stephanie

This edition published 1997 by Two-Can Publishing
in association with
Franklin Watts
96 Leonard Street
London EC2A 4RH

Hardback ISBN 1-85434-422-6

Dewey Decimal Classification 790.1

Printed in Spain by Graficromo S.A.

2 4 6 8 10 9 7 5 3 1

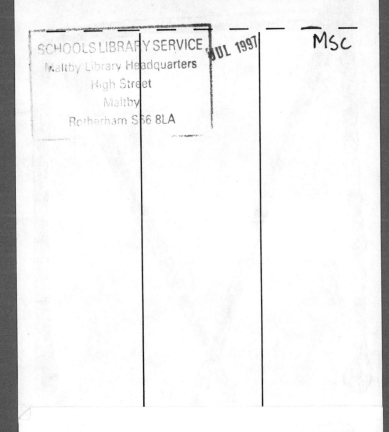

Contents

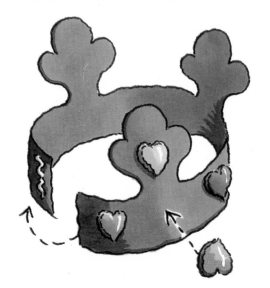

Being a princess was quite hard work, but lots of fun too! Living in a huge, stone castle could be a bit chilly but plenty of parties with delicious food made up for that! All princesses wore beautiful gowns and loads of precious jewels. Would you like to be a princess? *Yes! Well let's get started now...*

A princess had to get up extremely early in the morning. She needed lots of help to get dressed.

1 Tape the long sides of two sheets of wrapping paper together. Pleat the top edge and staple each fold in position. If you haven't got a stapler, use sticky tape.

First, she struggled into a long petticoat and a tight bodice. A richly embroidered gown went on top! You would never, ever have caught a princess wearing jeans and a T-shirt!

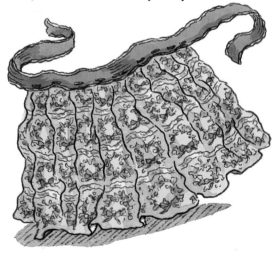

2 Neaten the waist edge by stapling or gluing on a length of ribbon. The ribbon should be longer than the skirt so that you can tie it around your waist.

6

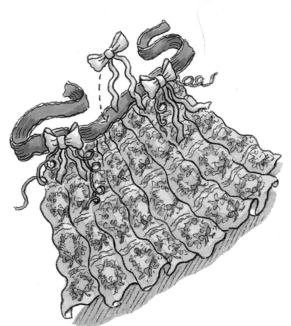

It's not that difficult being a princess – so far!

3 Tie some bows from ribbon and stick them to the waistband. They will cover up the glue or staples. Add brightly coloured streamers to finish off your skirt.

4 Cut the centre hole out of a paper doily. Snip through from the the middle to the outside edge. Slip the doily round your neck to make a beautiful collar.

O f course a princess had to have a crown! Because it was usually made from solid gold, the crown was very heavy. To stop it from falling off, the princess had to practise walking with a straight back and her head held high.

1 To make sure that your crown fits perfectly, measure round your head with a tape measure, or a piece of string. Add a bit extra to allow for an overlap.

This one seems to fit perfectly – as long as I don't bend down!

glue

glue

2 Use the measurement you have made to cut a crown shape from stiff card. Glue the ends together.

3 Now you can decorate your crown with coloured paper, sweets or shiny sequins.

I f there was one thing a princess loved more than anything else in the world, it was expensive jewellery – rich, red rubies, glittering garnets and sparkling sapphires.

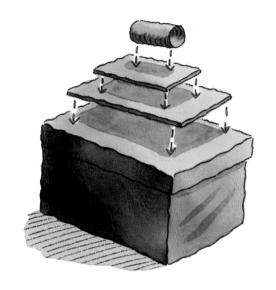

1 Find a strong cardboard box. A shoe box would be ideal. Glue two pieces of card on top of the lid – one slightly smaller than the other. Stick a small cardboard roll to the top!

She could never have enough necklaces, brooches and bangles. A special jewel box was a must for keeping everything safe.

2 Decorate the box by gluing on shapes torn, or cut, from coloured paper.

I hope she likes my gift, it cost all my pocket money!

3 Finish off your jewel box by gluing on brightly coloured sweets. They won't cost a fortune but will look like the real thing.

Princesses were expected to sit on beautiful – but very uncomfortable thrones – for hours on end. They had to listen to endless speeches and greet hundreds of visitors.

How they longed for a comfortable armchair to stop their bones from aching. But you couldn't be a proper princess without a throne!

1 Use a sturdy stool as the base for your throne. Find a large cardboard box to fit over the stool. You may have to cut the sides of the box down a little to make it fit.

2 Cut two cardboard shapes to fit over the sides of the box, and one for the back. Decorate each of the shapes with coloured paper.

3 Now glue the sides and the back in place. And most important of all, put a comfy cushion on the seat. Your throne is ready!

Time for a rest!

During the day a busy princess needed a break from speeches and visitors. What could be better exercise than a healthy gallop in the park? The princess chose her favourite horse and set off with her friends and pets. The cows were amazed!

1 Cut out all the pieces to make a horse's head. You'll need ears, nose, mouth and an eye.

3 Paint the eye, nose and mouth. Then glue them to the head, along with the ears. Glue on short lengths of thick string to make a hairy mane.

2 Next ask a grown-up to cut a slit in the top of a broomstick, deep enough to slot in your horse's head.

4 Now slot the horse's head into the slit in the broomstick. Jump on and gallop off!

A t the end of the day, when royal work was finished, the princess had time to enjoy herself.

1 To make a tambourine you'll need a strip of card about 50cm long and 8cm deep. Cut three holes about 5cm long and 2.5cm deep. Collect six metal bottle tops.

What she liked best was to listen to her favourite music. Musicians came to entertain the princess. She often joined in and sang and danced until it was time to eat!

2 Tape the ends of the card strip together. Cover the card circle with small pieces of newspaper and flour and water paste. Leave it to dry.

I've never played for a princess before!

3 Ask a grown-up to make holes in the bottle tops and thread through a short length of wire. Tape the wire and bottle tops to the inside of the holes. Take care with the sharp edges on the bottle tops. Cover the tape with more paste and paper.

4 Paint your tambourine in bright colours and patterns. Shake it around to join in with the rest of the band!

When the music was over, the princess had a delicious meal with all her friends. Nobody bothered to use knives and forks, fingers were fine! Royal pets joined in and helped chew on the bones. Drinks were served in jewelled goblets.

glue

1 Find some plastic or cardboard cups. Cut circles from card to make bases for your goblets. Glue the cups to the bases.

2 Paint rich, jewel-like patterns on the outside of your goblets. Acrylic paints will work best on plastic cups. Don't try to drink out of your goblets, just pretend!

O n special occasions a princess really enjoyed attending an exciting jousting tournament. Handsome knights on horseback charged and tried to knock each other off! The princess cheered loudly for her favourite horseman.

I've got a feeling that I'm going to win today

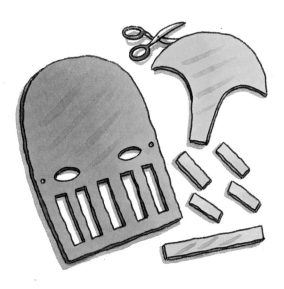

1 Cut out all the pieces for your knight's helmet from coloured card. Make holes for the eyes and long narrow slits so you can breathe and shout out loud!

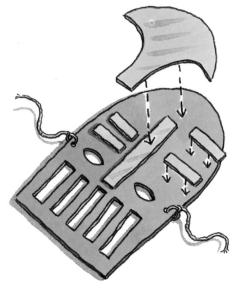

2 Glue on the pieces of card. Make small holes either side. Thread cord through. Knot the ends to stop them slipping through.

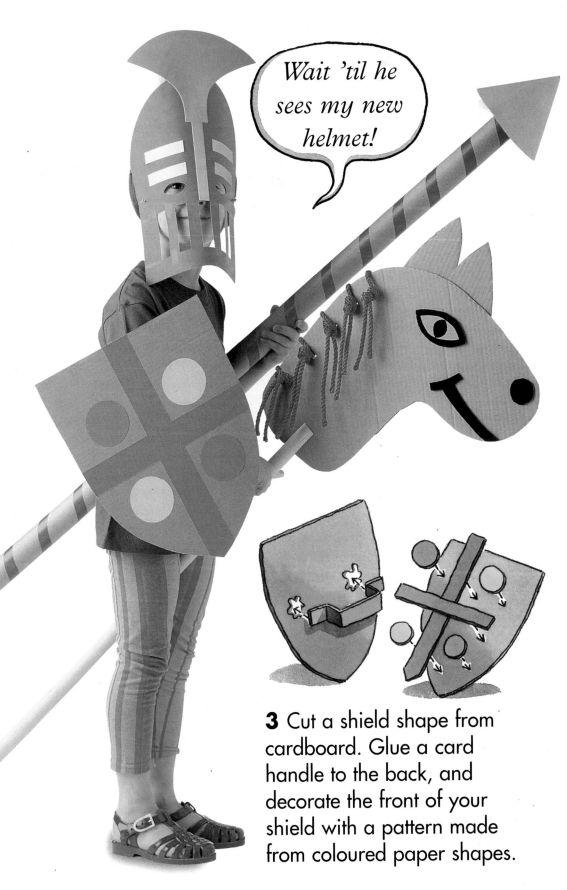

Wait 'til he sees my new helmet!

3 Cut a shield shape from cardboard. Glue a card handle to the back, and decorate the front of your shield with a pattern made from coloured paper shapes.

Every princess dreamed of sharing her life with a handsome, brave husband.
The wedding gave everyone in the royal palace a good excuse for holding a huge party to celebrate.
The musicians played, the court jester joked with the guests and the cook prepared a massive banquet.
It was the best day the princess had ever had in her life!

And EVERYONE lived very happily ever after!

Princesses used words that would sound very strange today! Here are a few to help you have a royal conversation. The words you would probably use today are underneath!

I pardon you with all my heart...

OK I forgive you

Trouble not yourself about that...

Don't worry, it'll be alright!

Why, how now, good mother...

Hi, mum!

I am sure some mischance will befall us...

We could be in trouble!

You have been long in coming...

Why are you so late?